PIP CAMPS OUT

Pip Camps Out

MYRA BERRY BROWN

Pictures by PHYLLIS GRAHAM

GOLDEN GATE JUNIOR BOOKS • San Carlos, California

For PIP
and his daddy, JOHN MICHAEL HAYES,
whose night together under the stars
inspired this story

Pip shouted and waved to his big sister.
He could see her in the back seat of the huge camp bus.
"Good-by, Lisa!" called Pip.

The bus started to go.
Everyone yelled and waved
to the screaming girls inside the bus.

Even Pip's dog, Wrangler,
pulled at his leash and barked.
"There they go!" said Daddy.

Mother said, "I hope I remembered
to put Lisa's name
on her sleeping bag!"
The top of the bus was loaded
with sleeping bags.
"Why can't I go to camp
and sleep in a sleeping bag?" asked Pip.
"You will some day," Mother told him.

Pip was still unhappy on the ride home.
"Everyone will be sleeping outside tonight,
except me," he complained.

After dinner Mother called
through the kitchen window,
"Pip! Pip!"
It was bedtime
but still light outside,
and Pip was playing somewhere.
Mother went to find him.

He wasn't swinging on the old tire
under the maple tree.

He wasn't in the shed
visiting Inky and her new kittens.

Daddy was up on a ladder
next to the shed
fixing something.
Mother asked, "Where's Pip?"
"He was just here," answered Daddy.
"He asked me to set his compass at North."

Mother had to stop to think
which way North was.
She walked out to the orchard.

First, she saw Daddy's old army canteen
under one of the apple trees—
and the flashlight
and the compass.

Then she saw Pip.
He was unrolling Daddy's old sleeping bag.
"What's all this?" asked Mother.
"I'm getting things ready," Pip told her.
"I'm going to sleep out here."
Wrangler barked.
"Wrangler'll stay with me."

Daddy came over
and Mother told him about it.
"Your son's getting ready
to sleep out here tonight."
Daddy thought it over.
"Hmmmm."
He looked at the sky
turning into twilight.
He knew how good it felt
to sleep out under the stars.
He said, "There's going to be
a beautiful moon tonight."

"And I'm sleeping right here—
where I can see it."
Pip had made up his mind.

Daddy turned to Mother.
"Why not?"
"It gets too cold and dark out here," said Mother.
"I'll wear my jacket," Pip promised.
"He could try it for a little while,"
said Daddy.
"He probably won't be able
to fall asleep anyway."
"Oh, yes, I will!" Pip declared.
"Well," said Mother, "I hope you know
what you're doing."

At the back door
Pip put on his warm jacket.
Mother patted his head
as she slipped two chocolate chip cookies
into his pocket.
"I hope you have a good night, Pip.
I'll leave this light on for you."

Pip ran all the way back to the orchard.
It was getting dark.
He pulled the sleeping bag out

where he could see the whole sky.
Then he sat down on it
and zipped up his jacket.

Wrangler curled up next to him.
Pip moved the flashlight
and the compass
and the canteen
closer.
When he saw the canteen
it made him thirsty.

He had to tip it high
or the water dripped down his neck.
"Want a drink, Wrangler?"
Wrangler's eyes were just closing.

Now, the night was all around him.

He switched on the flashlight
and a moth flew through its light.
"Everything's asleep out here,"
Pip thought to himself,
"everything—except me and the moth."

He stretched back flat
to see the whole sky.
Daddy was right.
There was a beautiful moon—
and so many stars.
He thought he saw a shooting star
but it turned out to be an airplane
with lights flashing on and off.

"I wonder where the North Star is?"
Pip sat up to work the compass,
but he couldn't find North by himself.

He wiggled far down into the sleeping bag
and pulled up its zipper.
Only his head and shoulders stuck out.
Now Pip was just like a real camper,
all ready for sleep.
But it was hard to feel sleepy
with clothes on—
especially shoes.

Mother's cookies!
He unzipped the sleeping bag a bit
to roll over
and get them out of his pocket.

The cookies were broken in little pieces
but they tasted good anyway.

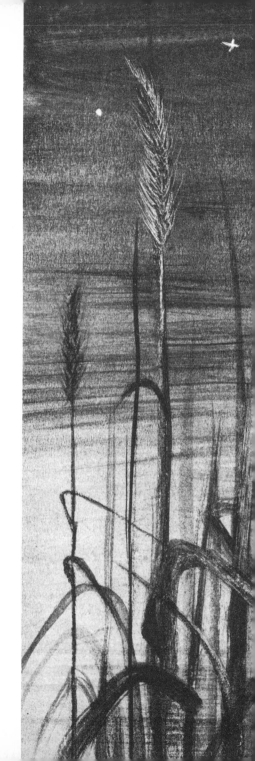

He heard the leaves crackling.
Pip sat up quickly and pointed his flashlight.
A gray squirrel was in the beam of light,
staring at Pip with big eyes.
Then it scurried away.

Pip lay down flat again.
The ground wasn't so soft as his own bed
in his own room.
He listened.
Chirrup. Chirrup. Chirrup.
Was that more than one cricket?
Was it two crickets—
or three—
or ten?

WHOOOOOOO! WHOOOOOOO!
That was an owl.
"A quiet night can be kind of noisy," thought Pip.

He looked back at the house
through the trees.
Yes, the light was still on.
Maybe Mother was already asleep.
Maybe Daddy too.
"I wonder if Lisa's asleep somewhere
right now
in her sleeping bag
under these same stars?"

Pip felt a lump in his pocket—
his harmonica.
He twisted over to take it out.
He blew a few notes.
It wasn't easy to play on the harmonica
lying down.
The music woke Wrangler.

The dog got up and stretched
and licked Pip's face
and rubbed next to him.
Then he lay down to sleep again.
Wrangler could fall asleep anywhere.
Suddenly Pip heard footsteps—
heavy footsteps.

Crunch. Crunch. Crunch.
Closer and closer!
Wrangler woke and barked.
Pip sat up straight.
He could feel his heart beating fast.

Daddy!
It was only Daddy—wearing his winter jacket
and carrying his sleeping bag.

"Well! How's the camper?" asked Daddy.
"Fine."
It was nice to see Daddy.
"Not asleep yet?" Daddy asked.
"Not yet."
Daddy said, "It's such a beautiful night
I decided to join you."
Pip smiled.

Daddy unrolled his sleeping bag
and sat down on it.
"Mother sent hot chocolate for us
in the thermos—a nightcap."

It was cozy
drinking hot chocolate with Daddy.

"What a night!" said Daddy.
"Where's that compass?"
Daddy could make a compass work.

"See? This is North," he showed Pip.
"There's the North Star."
He pointed far out.
"Over there's the Big Dipper,
and above us is the Milky Way."
Daddy knew the names of so many stars!

Pip yawned.
"Here," said Daddy,
"Mother sent you your pillow."
He tossed it to Pip.

The ground wasn't so hard after all.
Pip and his father
lay side by side
without talking.
Then his father asked,
"Any squirrels been by?"
"One," said Pip.
"Hear any owls?"
"Yes," said Pip.
"Any dinosaurs?"
Pip laughed.

"Where's your harmonica?"
The harmonica sounded better
when Daddy played it.
This time Wrangler only twitched his ears.
Daddy played *There's a Long, Long Trail*
and *Home on the Range.*
And then he played
In the Evening by the Moonlight.

That was the last song Pip heard.